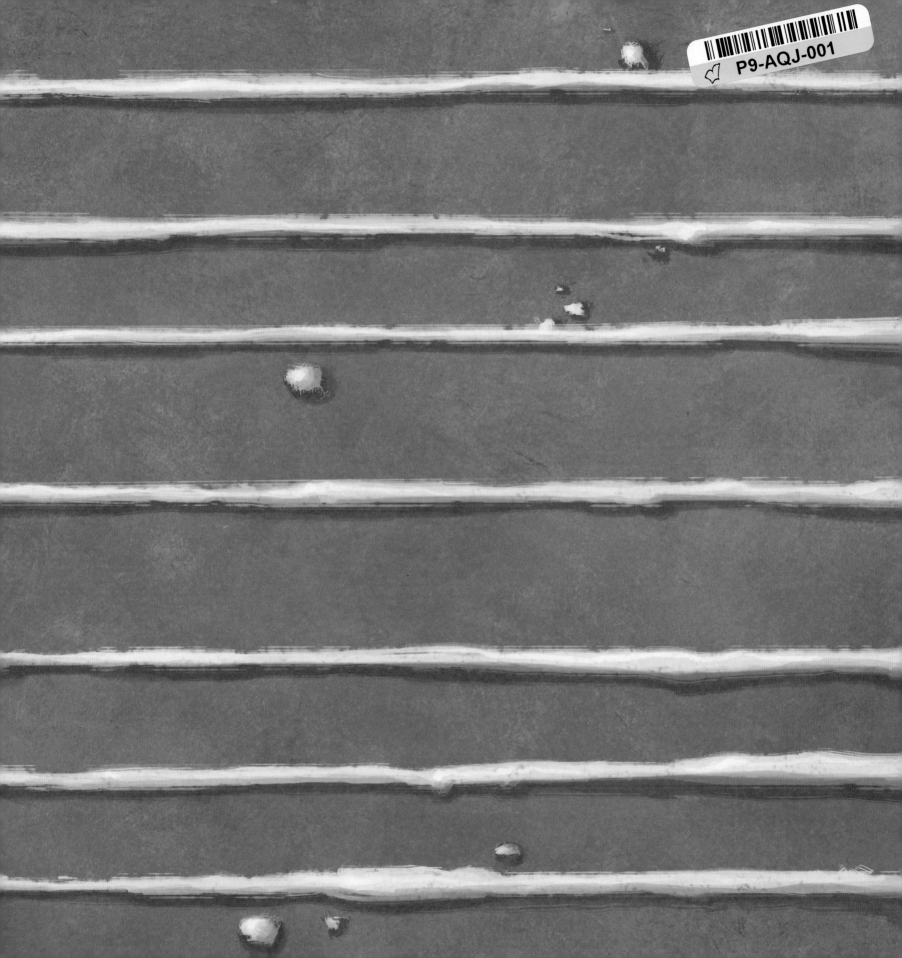

# Too Much Glue

Written by Jason Lefebvre

Illustrated by Zac Retz

Flash
Light PRESS

For my parents.
Thanks for everything you've done for me. —JL

Thank you family, for putting up with me
being an illustrator. —ZR

Printed in China. First Edition – September 2013
Library of Congress Control Number: 2013933388

ISBN 978-1-9362612-7-7

Editor: Shari Dash Greenspan
Graphic Design: The Virtual Paintbrush

This book was typeset in Hank.
The illustrations were rendered entirely
in Photoshop using custom brushes.

Distributed by IPG.
Flashlight Press, 527 Empire Blvd., Brooklyn, NY 11225
www.FlashlightPress.com

ART !!!

Our art teacher says,
   "Too much glue never dries."
She reminds us, "Glue raindrops, not puddles!"
And she warns me, "Matty, too much glue!"

But my dad and I love glue!
At home, we make glue
glasses, glue mustaches,
and even glue bouncy balls.
Mom is happy to help.

So during art class, I find the fullest bottles of glue.
I tip them over and squeeze. **Plooooop!**

Glue squishes from the orange tips and slops all over.
Sequins and googly eyes float around in a gluey lake.

Then it's time for the most important decoration...

I belly flop onto the table and roll around,
letting the glue and everything else cover me.

"Time to go on the drying rack!" I announce. But when I try to pull myself off the table, I boing right back down!

"Too much glue, Matty! Too much glue!" my teacher squawks.

This is bad. There's only half an hour until the end of school, and all I can do is lift my head, wave my hands, and wiggle my feet.

While my teacher breathes into a paper bag, Noah shouts, "Let's lasso him!"

Izzy, Noah, and Owen get to work.

Soon I'm roped from all sides like a rodeo pony.
But when they try to pull me out...

# SNAP!

The lassoes break, leaving colorful
octopus tentacles everywhere.

The glue is too
strong, and now
I'm a clingy
stringy, blucky
stucky mess.

"Don't worry, Matty. We know what to do!" shout Luke and Grace from across the room.

"Is that a tow truck?"
I ask as they wheel the
contraption over and
stick a plastic hook into
my suit of glue.

My friends pull one way and the glue pulls the other —
CREAK! CLICK! CREAK! CLICK! — until…

# KABOOOOM!

The tow truck explodes
and plastic bricks
rain all
over.

Now I'm a
clicky bricky,
clingy stringy,
blucky stucky mess.

The school nurse bursts in and checks my temperature. "98.6. Sorry. No fever. I can't send you home early."

She dabs and pats me like I'm spilled juice, but the more she blots,

the more the glue spreads.

Soon I'm a
melted mummy,
clicky bricky,
clingy stringy,
blucky stucky mess.

Then the principal comes in. He takes one look at me, sticks a note on my belly, and leaves.

Seeing my teacher huffing and puffing like a train gives me a great idea. I whisper it to Hailey and Owen.

The final bell rings and everyone freezes — except Owen and Hailey.

"It's the biggest one we could make!"
they shout, furiously flapping
a huge paper fan at me.

Then, just as I'm thinking I'll be a **note-on-my-tummy, melted mummy, clicky bricky, clingy stringy, blucky stucky glue boy** for the rest of my life, my plan works! Something my teacher said could never happen, happens: the glue dries!

But I'm still stuck, and now I hear footsteps... The door starts to open...

My father and some other carpool parents walk in. Dad comes closer and inspects me. Then he peels me off the table – glue, yarn, bricks, and all. He spins me around. No one makes a sound.

Then Dad smiles. "Matty, you're a masterpiece!"
He holds me up for everyone to admire.

My friends all cheer.

The car ride home is interesting.

Mom is speechless when Dad brings me in the house, but he knows just what to do. "Well, kiddo," Dad says, "some beautiful things only happen once, and this is one of those things." He gently grips the dried glue in front of my neck and behind my collar — and peels me open like a ripe banana!

Now it's Dad's turn to glue, and he seals up the sides of the me-shaped work of art.

"I bet it would take all the glue in the art room to make a YOU-shaped work of art, Dad!" I say.

Dad laughs. Then he glues a big magnet to the back of my project and hangs it on the fridge.

During dinner, we sneak peeks at my masterpiece. And **after** dinner...

...we take the principal's note very seriously.

FROM THE DESK OF
ELMER G. STUCKEY

Please encourage
Matty to use
tape instead
of glue.